Bonnybridge Primary School

Wellpark Terrace

Bonnybridge

Bonnybridge Primary School Library

Date Borrowed	Name	Date Returned

Also by Dick King-Smith:

Uncle Bumpo
Warlock Watson

Dick King-Smith
Bobby the Bad

Scholastic Children's Books,
Commonwealth House, 1-19 New Oxford Street,
London WC1A 1NU, UK
a division of Scholastic Publications Ltd
London – New York – Toronto – Sydney – Auckland

First published in the UK by Scholastic Ltd, 1994
This edition, 1995

Text copyright © Dick King-Smith/Foxbusters, 1994
Illustrations © Julie Anderson, 1994

ISBN 0 590 13278 4

Typeset by A J Latham, Houghton Regis, Dunstable, Beds

Printed by Cox & Wyman Ltd, Reading, Berks

10 9 8 7 6 5

Contents

1   Silly Old Miss Fox 1

2   Only an Old Spider 6

3   The Catapult 17

4   Pinching Other People's Stuff....................30

5   Superglue 42

6   The Man with the Upside-down Face.......54

7   Cows on the Pitch.....................................65

8   Ten out of Ten...75

9   Clint's Ear 87

10   Extra Strong Mints 99

11   A Broken Wrist 111

12   The Rescue...120

13   Good Old Foxy 128

Chapter 1

Silly Old Miss Fox

"Bobby Piff?" said Miss Fox.

There was no answer.

Perhaps he's absent, she thought, and caught herself secretly wishing that he was. If only he wasn't so bad, all the time.

"Bobby Piff!" she said again, loudly.

Bobby looked up from drawing a rather rude picture on the back of one of his neighbour's exercise books.

He smiled. "Yes?" he said.

Miss Fox put aside the thought that actually he had rather a sweet smile, and said, severely, "Yes, what?"

"Yes, Miss," said Bobby.

"Fox," said his teacher.

"Fox."

Miss Fox sighed, deeply.

"Tomorrow morning, Bobby," she said, "when I call your name, you will answer, 'Yes, Miss Fox,' Do you understand?"

"OK," said Bobby, returning to his drawing. "Yes, Miss Fox."

"Talking to yourself . . ." began Bobby.

"Bobby!" cried the teacher.

"Yes . . . Miss . . . Fox," said Bobby, just slowly enough to be quite maddening. "Talking to yourself," he said under his breath, "is the first sign of madness."

"What did you say, Bobby?" called Miss Fox.

"Nothing," said Bobby, and he smiled that rather sweet smile again.

After that things weren't too bad until morning break. Bobby kept fairly quiet, and seemed to be writing away quite happily. "You can all write me a story," Miss Fox had said. "My Best Day of the Holidays," and apart from saying, "How do we know which your best day was, Miss?" Bobby got on with it.

Walking around the classroom, Miss Fox took a peep at several of the stories. Bobby's effort didn't appear to have much to do with the title she had suggested. It seemed to be about some video he must have watched. She read . . .

" . . . and then the Destroyer blarsted the monster with his ray gun and blue off all its tentickles and there was a lot of blood."

After playtime things took a turn for the worse. A girl came in from the playground crying. Bobby Piff had pulled her pigtail.

A boy had scuffed knees. Bobby Piff had tripped him up.

And the Infant teacher, who had been on playground duty, looked in to say that she'd found one of her little ones in floods of tears and unable to move because, he said, a boy from Miss Fox's class had tied his shoelaces together.

"Bobby Piff!" said Miss Fox. "Was it you? Did you tie some little boy's shoelaces together?"

"I might of, Miss," said Bobby.

"I might *have*," said Miss Fox, automatically.

"Don't see how you could of," said Bobby.

"You weren't out in the playground."

"Bobby Piff! Go and stand in that corner!" screeched Miss Fox.

For some minutes Bobby stood still in the corner of the classroom, as deep in the corner as he could get. He shoved his nose into the angle where the two walls met and made a series of horrible faces. But then, getting bored with that, he began to inch his way, very very slowly, along one wall.

Miss Fox was writing on the blackboard and explaining something to the rest of the class, and she did not notice that Bobby had edged along until he could actually see out of the window nearest to the corner.

Now he put his mouth close to the window and started to blow long hot breaths on the glass, steaming it up. Then, with a finger, he began to draw a picture on the misty surface. Then he wrote something underneath.

So engrossed was he that he did not hear someone giggle, did not know that the teacher had put down her chalk and quietly come to stand immediately behind him.

Everyone else saw the teacher grab hold of Bobby Piff and march him out of the classroom, on the way to the Headmaster's office, but only those nearest could see, before it faded, the picture of a long thin matchstick figure with frizzy hair and a skirt, and under it the words,

Chapter 2

Only an Old Spider

"Had a nice day, Bobby?" said Mrs Piff when she came to collect her son that afternoon.

"All right," said Bobby.

He did not tell his mother that he had been kept in when the rest went out to play after lunch. Nor that the Headmaster, who was somewhat old-fashioned, had made him write out, "I must not be rude to Miss Fox" fifty times.

In fact, Bobby had only written this forty-eight times. With enjoyment he had left out one word in a couple of lines, which then read,

I must be rude to Miss Fox.

He reckoned the Headmaster wouldn't notice,

and indeed he hadn't. Nor did he mention to his mother the envelope in his anorak pocket, addressed to *Mr and Mrs Piff.*

"Give this note to your parents, Bobby," the Head had said as he licked the flap of the envelope and sealed it.

"OK," Bobby said.

"Less of your 'OK', young man," snapped the Head. "When I tell you to do something, you say 'Yes, sir'."

"Yes . . . sir," said Bobby.

No sir, he thought, when he hung up his anorak at home. He took out the envelope and considered whether he should

   a) burn it;

   b) tear it into little bits and put them in the dustbin;

   c) tear it into little bits and flush them down the toilet;

   d) put it back in his pocket and pretend to forget about it: maybe the Head would forget, too;

 or e) steam it open and see what the note said.

He quickly decided on Plan e). Plan e) meant that he could satisfy his curiosity and still settle on Plans a), b), c), or d) afterwards.

He filled the electric kettle with hot water, and switched it on. His mother came into the kitchen.

Bobby got out the teapot.

"What are you doing, Bobby?" asked Mrs Piff. "Why is the kettle switched on? You shouldn't mess with kettles, they can be dangerous."

With one hand Bobby held out the teapot. He smiled sweetly. "I was going to make a cup of tea for you, Mum," he said. "It's not teatime yet," his mother said.

"I just thought you might like an early one, Mum."

Never before had Mrs Piff received such an offer from her son. And I might never again, she thought; better make hay while the sun shines.

Once she was out of the way and the kettle had begun to boil, Bobby held down the cut-off switch with one hand while with the other he passed the back of the envelope to and fro before the steady plume of steam coming from the kettle's spout.

Then he made a pot of tea, took a cup out to his wondering mother and, shutting himself in his room, lifted the now unstuck flap of the envelope and carefully took out the Headmaster's note.

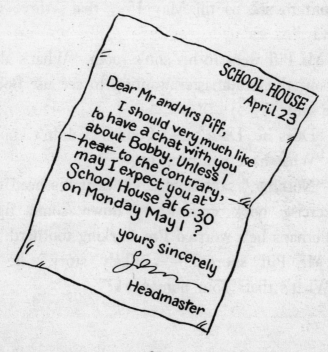

SCHOOL HOUSE
April 23

Dear Mr and Mrs Piff,
I should very much like to have a chat with you about Bobby. Unless I hear to the contrary, may I expect you at School House at 6.30 on Monday May 1 ?

yours sincerely

Headmaster

At this point Bobby decided on a new plan, Plan f). He found a biro – black, the same colour as the writing on the note – and wrote in a *5* after *May 1*. Then he refolded the note, put it back in its envelope, gummed up the flap, and took the letter to his mother.

"Forgot to give you this," he said.

"Bobby's headmaster sent a note," said Mrs Piff to her husband when he returned from work. "He wants to see us about Bobby."

"Why, what's he been up to?" said Mr Piff.

"Don't know. Can't be anything bad. He doesn't want to see us till May 15 – that's three weeks away."

Mr Piff went to his son's room. "What's all this about the headmaster wanting to see us, Bobby?" he said.

"Does he, Dad?" said Bobby. "I didn't know."

"What have you been up to?"

"Nothing," said Bobby. He bent his head to his exercise book and wrote down some figures. "Perhaps he's worried I'm working too hard."

Mr Piff snorted. "A likely story," he said. "What's that? Your homework?"

Bobby nodded. "Maths," he sighed. "These sums are ever so hard, but I'm doing my best."

His father looked.

"They're certainly not easy," he said. "Let's see. Yes, that's right . . . and so's that . . . and that. Blow me down, Bobby, you've got them all right so far!"

Bobby looked up, smiling. "Have I, Dad?" he said.

"Yes," said Mr Piff. "Can't think how," he added.

Little did he know that hidden under one of Bobby's comics was Miss Fox's Answer Book. Little did Miss Fox know, when she came to correct the class's maths homework next day, that her Answer Book had been removed from her desk and then replaced again.

The day had started oddly for her anyway, for when she read the register and came to Bobby's name, he answered "Yes, Miss Fox" immediately. And he didn't pull anyone's hair in break or trip anyone up or tie anybody's shoelaces together, and when Miss Fox was correcting the homework in her lunch hour, she had an even bigger shock.

Every one of Bobby Piff's answers was right!

She sent for him.

"Bobby," she said. "Did your father or your mother help you with these sums?"

"Oh no, miss!" said Bobby. "I done them all myself."

"You *did* them all yourself."

"That's what I just said."

"Are you telling the truth?"

"I always does."

"You always *do*."

"Yes."

It's too good to be true, said Miss Fox to herself, but I mustn't show my doubts. Perhaps he just needs encouragement. "Well done, Bobby!" she said. "I can see that you're going to be trying very hard this term."

I hope, she thought, though more likely he's just going to be very trying.

In fact Bobby wasn't too bad for the rest of that day.

To be sure, in the middle of reading time, when the class was meant to be quite quiet and the teacher's back was turned as she wrote on the blackboard, somebody made a sudden rude noise that set everyone giggling.

But when Miss Fox whipped round, Bobby's nose was deep in his book. I won't accuse him, she thought, he's been so good today. Perhaps that talking-to he got from the Head has had an effect. Perhaps Bobby's going to turn over a new leaf.

Unfortunately the day was spoiled for her in quite a different way. Miss Fox was terrified of spiders. None of the children knew this, for on the occasions when she had seen one in the classroom, she had managed to control herself.

But that afternoon, when she opened the stock cupboard to get some paper, there, right by her outstretched hand, was a huge spider. It was big enough to have given Miss Muffet forty fits, let alone Miss Fox, who slammed the cupboard door and retreated, white-faced.

"What's the matter?" everyone cried.

"Oh!" said Miss Fox. "A spider! A great big one! Will someone please catch it and get rid of it?"

"Me, Miss! Me, Miss! Me!" they all said, but Bobby Piff was off his chair and into the cupboard like a flash. He came out with his hands cupped

together.

"Got him," he said.

"Take it outside, Bobby, please," said Miss Fox.

"It's only an old spider," Bobby said.

Fascinated, the class watched the short sturdy figure of Bobby Piff advancing upon the tall lanky figure of Miss Fox, who backed hastily away.

"Stay where you are, Bobby!" she cried. "Don't come a step nearer. I can't stand the sight of spiders!"

"It won't hurt you," Bobby said. "They don't."

"Take it outside," said Miss Fox faintly, "and get rid of it."

"You want me to kill it?" said Bobby.

"Yes! Yes! No, no, I mean I don't care what you do with it. Let it go in the playground. Just take it out, d'you hear?"

"OK," said Bobby.

Outside the classroom he slowly opened his cupped palms. The big spider sat there on its eight big legs.

"Don't worry," said Bobby. "I'm not going to kill you. I like spiders. And I'm not going to put you out in the playground either. You might catch cold. You stay inside, in the warm. And I shouldn't go back into our classroom if I were you, she might squash you." He put it down on the floor.

"So she can't stand the sight of spiders!" said Bobby as it scuttled away. "More likely you couldn't stand the sight of old Miss Fox."

Chapter 3

The Catapult

Miss Fox came to school next day in a very nervous state. She did not especially mind that the other children in the class now knew of her fear of spiders – it might lead to an interesting discussion at some time. She could talk about other phobias – of heights, of snakes, of the dark, or of flying in aeroplanes – and why people had them, and what could be done about it. No, what mattered to her was that Bobby Piff knew.

For him it would be quite simple – she could just imagine what he must be thinking. "Miss Fox is frightened of spiders. So now I know how to frighten Miss Fox. I'll catch loads of spiders and let them go in the classroom." Or on my desk, she thought. Or on me! She shuddered at the idea of a spider's eight feet on the flesh of her arm. He'll probably come into school with a box full of them, she said to herself, and it was with something like terror that she saw Bobby Piff enter the classroom and walk straight up to her desk.

"What do you want?" she said.

"I just come to say," said Bobby, "that if you find any more of those old spiders, I'll catch 'em for you and get rid of 'em."

"Oh thank you, thank you, Bobby," said Miss Fox.

I misjudged him, she thought; and indeed for the rest of that first week Bobby was no trouble at all. Or rather he was no trouble to Miss Fox, though other teachers and other children might have had to suffer, as usual, from the worrisome ways of Bobby Piff.

On the following Monday, the first day of May, the Headmaster said to Miss Fox, "How is that bad boy, Bobby Piff? I've got his parents coming to see me this evening."

"Well, it's funny," said Miss Fox, "but apart from that first day of term he's been pretty good. And he seems to be working, too – the other day he did every single sum of his maths homework correctly."

"Hm," said the Head. "I've never yet heard of a leopard changing its spots."

When 6.30 came and went with no sign of the Piffs, he rang them up. Bobby answered the phone.

"Dad!" he called. "It's old . . . it's the Head. For you."

Mr Piff took the phone and Bobby went out of the room.

"I wondered," said the Head, ". . . have you been delayed?"

"Delayed?" said Mr Piff.

"Yes. I was expecting you and your wife at 6.30."

"On May 15," said Mr Piff. "That's what it said on your note."

"Are you sure?"

"Certain. Hang on, I've got it here somewhere . . . yes, here we are . . . 'May I expect you at

School House at 6.30 on Monday May 15.' That's not for another two weeks."

The Headmaster scratched his head. "I can't think why I wrote that," he said.

"What's the trouble?" asked Mr Piff. "Bobby been a nuisance or something?"

He's never anything else, thought the Head, but then he remembered Miss Fox's recent report.

"No, no," he said. "Not really."

He thought quickly. According to his teacher, the boy's behaviour had improved. So maybe, even though leopards were stuck with their spots, it might be better to let sleeping dogs lie.

"Look, I'm sorry, Mr Piff," he said. "I seem to have made a muddle of this. We'll forget all about it for the time being."

"OK," said Mr Piff. "Glad to hear Bobby's behaving himself."

"Ah. Yes. Quite," said the Headmaster.

Outside the room, Bobby took his ear from the keyhole and went softly up the stairs to his room. Whatever the old Head was on about, it didn't sound too bad. He settled down to some target practice.

Bobby had bought a little catapult, small enough to go into a trouser pocket, and just the job for shooting pill-sized pellets of tightly rolled up paper. He planned to fire this weapon in class, once he had become skilled enough in its use.

There were a number of children he proposed to shoot – mostly goody-goodies who were forever sucking up to Miss Fox, or the kind of sneaks who, whenever the teacher asked, "Who did that?" or "Who said that?" always answered "Bobby Piff!" whether it was or it wasn't.

It would be fun to have a pot at old Miss Fox, he thought. But, reckoning this might not be wise, he had instead drawn a large picture and stuck it on one wall of his room with Blu-Tack, to act as a target.

To anyone else the picture appeared to be of a dog, a prick-eared dog with rather a bushy tail, but in fact it was Bobby's impression of a fox (a female one).

He had just fired a couple of shots at it when he heard his father coming up the stairs. He

slipped the catapult into his pocket and opened a book.

"Doing your homework?" Mr Piff asked.

"In the middle of it, Dad," said Bobby.

"Good. Give it your best shot."

"I will," said Bobby when his father had gone, and he aimed carefully and scored a bullseye on the fox.

On the following three evenings Bobby put in some intensive catapult-homework, and on the Friday of that week he went to school with the secret weapon in his pocket.

Normally he paid little attention when Miss Fox was reading the register, but now he listened carefully to the other children's names, sorting out in his mind who should be the first target. He was still thinking deeply about this when his own name was called, and he did not answer it.

Oh, no, thought Miss Fox, it's going to be one of those days.

"Bobby Piff," she said again, loudly.

"Yes."

"Yes what?"

"Yes, Miss."

"Yes, Miss Fox."

"Yes . . . Miss . . . Fox," said Bobby with a smile.

When you're standing with your back turned, writing on the blackboard, he thought, I bet I could hit you smack on the . . . Better not, though, some creep'd tell on me.

He decided on his first victim, a boy he'd never liked. Not that he liked any of them much, boys or girls, though he preferred those who would fight back when he thumped them. There were three or four such boys, and a big girl of eleven with a quick temper, but he picked on the creepiest of the creeps, called Kevin. Like a skilled hunter who stalks his prey, Bobby bided his time until conditions were just right.

They were practising for a concert, with Miss Fox playing the piano, in the school hall. Bobby positioned himself at the back of the class. He was just at the right range, behind and slightly to one side of Kevin, with a clear field of fire between other children, and he waited till the singing was at its loudest.

Then, stealthily, he took the catapult from his

pocket, fitted into its little pouch a large and very tightly rolled paper pellet, drew back the elastic to its full stretch, and fired.

Over the sound of the singing came a shrill yell.

Miss Fox stopped playing and stood up.

"Who made that noise?" she cried.

"Bobby Piff," said several voices automatically, but Kevin, his hand clapped to his head, wailed, "I did! Someone hit me on the ear!"

Instinctively Miss Fox looked at Bobby standing innocently at the back of the class – much too far from Kevin, she judged, to have thrown something at him.

"Look, Miss!" said a girl, picking up the paper pellet from the floor. "It was this."

Miss Fox held it between finger and thumb.

"Who threw this at Kevin?" she said.

"Bobby Piff," said the voices again.

"Bobby?" said Miss Fox. "Did you throw this pellet at Kevin?"

"No," said Bobby, with some truth. After all, he had shot it, not thrown it. "I never done it," he said.

"I never *did* it," said Miss Fox.

"You couldn't of," said Bobby. "You were playing the piano."

The singing continued. Once again there was another sharp yelp, this time from the big girl with the temper; once again Bobby was the prime suspect, and once again nothing could be proved against him, for no-one had actually seen the catapult. But after Miss Fox had said, "Come and stand here, by the piano, Bobby," there were, she noticed, no more yelps.

At midday she had what she, mistakenly, thought was a good idea. There was to be painting after lunch. If I get Bobby to put out the painting materials, she thought, at least he won't be able to get into mischief in the playground and I can keep my eye on him. He'll have to do it on his own. If I get other children to help him, he's sure to throw water at them or, worse, paint.

Bobby was not too pleased to be given this duty. He'd planned a little rough shooting in the playground, picking off a few of his pet hates while the dinner ladies weren't watching. But as he worked, mixing up the brightly-coloured paints, he had what he, mistakenly, thought was a good idea.

At present the ammunition for his catapult was all solid shot. How much better if it was high-explosive!

Choosing the brightest of the colours (a brilliant red – it'll look like blood, he thought), he concocted a really gooey blend of paint and water, rolled up a sizeable pellet of paper, and proceeded thoroughly to soak it in the mixture.

"Have you finished, Bobby?" called Miss Fox from her desk where she was marking some work.

"Nearly," said Bobby, throwing her one of his smiles. "Nearly ready."

"Well, I'm going to have a cup of coffee in the Staff Room now," said his teacher. "Thank you very much for your help. Go out and play when you've done."

"OK," Bobby said.

He waited till he was alone in the classroom and then fitted the well-soaked pellet to his catapult and fired at a window. It burst with a most satisfying squelch.

Bobby looked at the clock. Nearly time for the bell, he thought. They'll be coming back into the classroom soon. I'll ambush the first one through the door.

He made another pellet, soaked it in his bright red mixture, and took up a firing position, behind the open door.

As the bell rang and the children began to stream into the building from the playground, the Headmaster came out of his office and

walked down the corridor towards Miss Fox's classroom.

I'd better have a word with her about Bobby Piff, he said to himself. See how he's getting on.

It was a pity that he was wearing a newish light-coloured suit and a white shirt and a smart tie his wife had given him for his birthday, because as he came through the doorway, the patent Piff high-explosive imitation-blood bullet hit him squarely in the chest.

Chapter 4

Pinching Other People's Stuff

The children of Miss Fox's class, arriving at their usual gallop, suddenly stopped dead in their tracks.

There, in the middle of their classroom, stood the Headmaster, his white shirt stained with a great splash of scarlet, his suit and his tie bespattered with drops of what looked like . . . could it be?

"Oh! Oh! *Oh!*" they cried, and when Miss Fox came hurrying to see what all the noise was about, they shouted "He's been shot!"

"Who's been shot?" said Miss Fox, pushing through them.

"The Headmaster."

"Who shot him?"

"Bobby Piff!"

"Oh! Oh! *Oh!*" cried Miss Fox, her mind in a whirl. "Oh, whatever has happened?"

"Be quiet, all of you!" roared the Head (and 'all', it seemed, included Miss Fox), "and sit down in your places immediately."

Everyone sat down, including Miss Fox, except Bobby who could not, since the Head had hold of his collar with one hand, while in the other he held the catapult.

"Now then," said the Headmaster, "there has been a little accident," (they all held their breath) "with some red paint," (they all let it out again) "and you will be glad to hear that I am not bleeding to death." (They all looked very relieved, except Bobby, who appeared disappointed.) "I see you're all ready to do some painting, Miss Fox, so I won't delay you any longer. Come, Bobby."

"I asked Bobby to mix the paints up for me," said Miss Fox, "I'm afraid."

"*I'm* afraid," said the Head, "that Bobby himself got a little mixed up. He and I are just going to have a chat about it all." And, keeping a firm grip on Bobby Piff, out he went.

Seated opposite the Headmaster in his office, Bobby eyed the damage done by the patent Piff bullet.

Bullseye, he thought, and talk about high-explosive! Wonder what the old Head'll do? He can't beat me, they're not allowed to nowadays.

"Now, Bobby," said the Headmaster, and his voice was dangerously quiet, "where did you get this?" and he laid the catapult on his desk.

"Bought it."

"Sir."

"Sir."

"You must have known you're not allowed to bring such a thing into school."

"Nobody never told me . . . Sir."

"Nobody *ever* told you."

"That's right."

The Headmaster sighed. "Catapults are dangerous weapons," he said. "If you fired a stone from it, you could hit someone in the eye."

"I could," said Bobby. "I'm pretty good, I am. But I was only shooting bits of paper."

"Which you had soaked in paint."

"Yes."

The Headmaster looked long and hard at Bobby.

"I'm going to give you credit," he said, "for being able to tell the truth when it really matters. Did you fire that paint-soaked pellet at me on purpose?"

"No, I never," said Bobby. "I was just going to shoot the first one through the door. I didn't know it was going to be you. Honest." He smiled. "Sorry," he said.

The Headmaster put aside the thought that actually he had rather a sweet smile. "Right, Bobby," he said. "I will take your word for that. But I am very displeased with your behaviour and I shall punish you for shooting off that catapult in school. Also I shall speak to your parents about you."

I'd like to beat you, he thought, but we're not allowed to nowadays.

"You will not bring the thing into school ever again," he said. "Do you understand?"

"OK," said Bobby. "Please Sir," he said, "can

I have it back now?"

"You most certainly cannot," said the Head. "I am confiscating it." He opened the top drawer of his desk and dropped the catapult in.

The Piffs' telephone rang that evening, and after some while Bobby's father came upstairs to his room and shut the door behind him.

"Right," he said. "I know all about this business with the catapult and the paint, and I know what punishments you've been given, so I'm not going to give you any more. But of course I had to offer to settle the bill for cleaning the Headmaster's clothes. Except that I'm not paying it – you are. No more pocket money till it's paid off, understand?"

Bobby looked up from his homework. Fortunately it was maths, and fortunately he had managed to nick the Answer Book again.

"OK, Dad," he said, "but what about my catapult?"

"What about it?"

"He's got it."

"Quite right, too."

"But it's mine, Dad. It belongs to me. He ought to give it back."

"I expect he will, one day, when you start behaving better. If that day ever comes. You'd better make up your mind to start to be a better boy, my son. From what the Head's been telling me, you're becoming a really bad boy."

By the time Bobby had finished copying in the

correct answers to his homework, he had made up his mind about one thing. He would rescue his catapult.

What right had the old Head to keep it? It doesn't belong to him, it belongs to me, said Bobby to himself. I paid for it, with my own money, and now he's taken it off me. That's stealing, that is, that's wrong: he ought to be punished, he ought, stealing other people's property. I'll get it back, he thought, as he put the property that *he* had stolen, the Answer Book, in his satchel, ready to slip it back in Miss Fox's desk next morning. I'll get in that old office and I'll take it out of his desk. It's mine, not his. Before he fell asleep that night, Bobby's plans were laid. They were simple, he thought.

If he was to go into the Head's office, the Head mustn't be there. So he must be certain the Head was somewhere else. Where? In the hall, taking Assembly. Everybody would be in Assembly. Everybody, he said to himself, but one.

Next morning Miss Fox's children trooped out of their classroom behind her on their way to the hall, all but one, the last out, who dodged back in again.

Bobby waited until the sound of music told him that Assembly had started, and then he nipped quickly along the corridor to the Headmaster's office, opened the door and went in.

Straight to the desk he went and pulled at the top drawer. It was locked. On the desk, Bobby saw, there were some keys, but they didn't fit the drawer when he tried. He put them in his pocket and slipped out of the office.

When Miss Fox's children came back into the classroom, Bobby, who had been standing behind the open door, joined them unnoticed.

In fact, as luck would have it, no one had noticed that he had not been in Assembly.

The Headmaster was too occupied with the little talk he was giving (about the importance of honesty, and how you must never ever take other people's possessions).

Miss Fox was too busy, playing the piano for the hymns.

And Miss Fox's class were all in a daydream, thinking about what was for lunch or what would be on telly that evening or other such interesting subjects.

All Bobby was thinking about was his catapult.

It was bad enough that it had been stolen from him, but now to have it locked away – that was really wrong. That old Head, he ought to be reported to the police, pinching other people's stuff and not letting them pinch it back.

He fingered the keys in his pocket.

At morning break the Headmaster said to his deputy, "I'm off to a Heads' Meeting – I'll be back after lunch."

He looked on his desk for his car keys. They were not there.

"I could have sworn I left them there," he said.

He fumbled in his pockets. Things are getting on top of me, he thought, what with putting the wrong date in that letter to the Piffs, and now losing my keys. It must be the strain of having to cope with someone like that Bobby Piff. How am I going to get to this meeting? Perhaps I dropped them somewhere on my way in this morning.

He left his office and went out through the playground on his way to the car park, looking all about on the ground.

"Lost something?" said the teacher who was on playground duty.

"My car keys," said the Head. "I must have dropped them."

One of the children near enough to have heard this chanced to be Bobby Piff.

Choosing a moment when no one was looking, Bobby took the keys from his pocket and let

them fall. He waited a bit and then he shouted, "Sir! Sir! I've found them!"

The Headmaster hurried back, to see Bobby pointing to the ground. "Look, there's your keys," said Bobby. "I just heard you say you lost 'em and I started looking and there they were."

Once again the Headmaster looked long and hard at Bobby. Wild suspicions flashed through his mind, that somehow Bobby Piff had stolen his car keys from his office desk and then, just now, taken them out of his pocket and thrown them down on the playground. What a crazy idea, he told himself, I must be losing my reason. He picked up the keys.

"Thank you, Bobby," he said. "I'm grateful to you."

Bobby smiled.

"Well then," he said, "can I have my catapult now?"

"Certainly not," said the Head. He looked at his watch and hurried off to his car.

"OK," said Bobby under his breath. "But you just wait. I'll get my own back."

Chapter 5

Superglue

Life, thought Bobby, was just not fair. Look at all the good things he'd done already this term.

He'd saved old Miss Fox from a spider.

He'd mixed up all her paints for her.

He'd got two lots of maths homework right, every single sum.

And he'd found – well, sort of found – the old Head's rotten old car keys.

And what thanks had he got for all that lot? A load of punishments and his catapult stolen, and his pocket money stopped. How do they expect me to behave better when they treat me like that, he said to himself. There's not much point in trying to be good. I might just as well be bad. It's more fun anyway. He began the very next day.

Miss Fox, seeing Bobby Piff arrive for school with a face like thunder, quailed inwardly.

"Good morning, Bobby," she said brightly, hoping perhaps for that smile of his, but all he said was, "Is it?"

"That's not a very polite way to speak," said Miss Fox.

"Isn't it?" said Bobby.

"No, it is not!" said Miss Fox angrily. And it's not going to be a good morning, she thought, I can see that a mile off.

How right she was.

First, getting him to answer his name properly was even worse than ever, for instead of the usual "Yes" and then "Yes, Miss", he shouted "YES, MISS FOX!" so loudly that it started the class giggling.

Then, in Assembly, there were more giggles coming from the neighbourhood of Bobby Piff, the cause of which Miss Fox, at the piano, could not determine. Until Kevin told her afterwards.

"It was Bobby, Miss," he said, back in the classroom. "He was singing rude words to the hymn."

"Bobby!" said Miss Fox. "Is this true?"

"Yes, Miss Fox!" said Bobby, again very loudly.

"D'you know what he said?" went on Kevin. "He said . . ."

"That will do, Kevin," said Miss Fox. "Bobby, I will talk to you about this later."

"OK," said Bobby.

You wait, he thought, you're going to have lots to talk about. Up until break he contented himself by being annoying. First he kept moving his chair about, so that its legs squeaked on the floor.

"Who is that squeaking their chair?" said Miss Fox.

"Bobby Piff!" they said.

"Sit still, Bobby."

"Sorry, Miss. I got cramp in my leg."

Then he began to sniff, loudly, at intervals of a quarter of a minute.

"Who is that sniffing?" asked Miss Fox.

"Bobby Piff!" they said.

"Blow your nose, Bobby."

"Haven't got a hanky, Miss."

"Well, stop sniffing."

"Got a bad cold, Miss."

Then he swapped the sniff for a cough, a hor-rid hacking cough, so loud that Miss Fox had no need to ask whose it was.

"Sorry, Miss," said Bobby, after the twentieth cough. "It's my cold. I'm not very well. I ought to be at home."

I wish to Heaven you were, thought the teacher.

"Go and have a drink of water," she said.

In the boys' washroom, Bobby filled a basin with water. Then he went along the line of pegs where the coats were hung, found Kevin's anorak, gave it a thorough soaking in the basin, and hung it up again. As an afterthought, he left the plug in and turned the tap on full.

At break time Miss Fox said, "Put your coats on, everyone, it's quite cold today."

When the others went out, Bobby lurked behind in the classroom just long enough to hear Kevin's squawks of surprise as he put his anorak on, and to slip Miss Fox's Answer Book back in her drawer. For good measure, he put a drawing-pin, point up, on the seat of Kevin's chair.

At the end of break Miss Fox came back from the Staff Room just in time to see Kevin sit down and leap up again like a pilot ejecting, and to hear a chorus of voices telling her that some-one had soaked Kevin's anorak, and that some-one had left a tap running and the washroom floor was flooded, and that someone had put a drawing-pin on Kevin's chair.

Miss Fox took a deep breath.

"Bobby Piff," she said. "Did you do all these things?"

"Yes, he did!" everyone cried.

Bobby preserved a dignified silence.

"Well?" said Miss Fox. "Did you? Did you get Kevin's anorak wet?"

"I expect it was still wet from yesterday," Bobby said. "It was raining yesterday."

"And what about the water on the washroom floor?"

"I might of forgotten to turn the tap off when you sent me out to get a drink," said Bobby. "Like I told you, I wasn't feeling well. I might of had a little bit of a blackout."

"And the drawing-pin? I suppose you're going to tell me Kevin put a drawing-pin on the seat of his chair and then sat on it?"

"He might of," said Bobby. "He's stupid enough."

"Go and stand in the corner," said Miss Fox. "That one," she said, remembering the first day of term and pointing to a corner that was nowhere near a window.

Bobby got up, scowling.

"You're always picking on me," he said.

"One more word from you," said Miss Fox, "and I shall send you straight to the Headmaster."

"*He's* always picking on me, too," muttered Bobby.

"And don't mutter like that!"

"Next thing, she'll be telling me not to breathe," said Bobby out of the corner of his mouth as he made his way across the room, and Kevin, who happened to hear this, said "Good job, too."

Miss Fox waited till Bobby was standing, silent, in the corner. "Now," she said to the class, "perhaps we can get on with the lesson."

Now, she thought, I suppose he'll start sniffing again.

He did.

Miss Fox carried on bravely, though she felt sure that soon the coughing would begin.

It did.

I'm not going to say anything to him, she

thought, raising her voice and hoping that the class was listening to her. He'll only tell me he's got a bad cold.

Then she became aware that, though Bobby's back was turned to her, his arm was raised.

"What is it, Bobby?" she said.

"Can I go to the toilet?" he asked.

"No, certainly not," she said. "You can wait till the end of the lesson."

"I might not be able to," said Bobby to the wall, and the usual sniggers broke out.

For a while neither sniff nor cough came from him, and Miss Fox breathed an inward sigh of relief. She should have known better.

Suddenly, as she wrote on the blackboard, there came from the corner a loud "Hic!" and she turned in time to hear it followed by a second. And not only to hear it but to see it, for Bobby's acting of an attack of hiccups was theatrical, to say the least. At each "Hic!" his shoulders shot up and his body jerked back from the wall as though he had been struck by a bullet. It all looked quite genuine: there was no way to tell that it wasn't. And there was no way

to teach twenty-nine children while the thirtieth was making such a row.

"Try holding your breath, Bobby," said Miss Fox.

"I told you," muttered Bobby to those nearest. "I *said* she'd – hic! – tell me to stop breathing." Aloud he said, "Please, Miss – hic! – Fox, it's standing up that – hic! – does it."

"Oh sit down, do!" cried Miss Fox desperately.

And the moment that Bobby sat down, oddly enough, the hiccuping stopped completely.

At lunchtime Miss Fox persuaded herself that perhaps she should postpone giving Bobby Piff a good talking-to until the end of the day. For one thing, she found, as she sat in the Staff Room correcting homework, that once again Bobby had got every one of his sums right. And who knows, she thought, he might behave better this afternoon. Little did she know what the afternoon was to bring.

Just before the bell went for the end of the midday break, Miss Fox returned to her classroom to find Bobby alone there, seated at his table, writing busily.

"Why aren't you out playing?" she said.

"Got to do this writing for the Head," Bobby said.

"A punishment, you mean?"

"Yes, and me not feeling well either." He gave a graveyard cough.

Oh dear, thought soft-hearted Miss Fox, maybe he isn't well. He looks so unhappy.

But Bobby's looks belied his feelings. In his heart he was as happy as could be. Not long now, he thought. What a bit of luck to have

found that tube of stuff in old Miss Fox's cupboard.

The bell rang, and the children came back into
the classroom.

"Sit down, all of you," said Miss Fox, and she
lowered herself into her own chair.

Then, by sheer chance, there was a knock on
the door and there stood the Headmaster with a
man and a woman.

"Excuse me, Miss Fox," he said. "I'm just
showing these new parents around the school.
May we come in?"

"Of course!" cried Miss Fox. "Stand up, children, stand up, all of you."

And up they all stood, and so did Miss Fox,
with her chair firmly stuck to her with
Superglue.

Chapter 6

The Man with the Upside-down Face

"If Bobby continues in this way," said the Headmaster to Mr and Mrs Piff that evening, "I may be forced to put the whole matter before the School Governors. It may be that Bobby is too big a problem for us to deal with."

"D'you mean you'd expel him?" said Mr Piff.

"It could come to that."

"He's no trouble at home," said Mrs Piff.

"Really?" said the Head. "It would appear, then, that he saves it up for us. He is no respecter of persons, your son. We all suffer: the other children, myself, Miss Fox especially. Today has been a prime example – Bobby at his worst all morning and then this episode with the glue. It was all the more unfortunate that I was showing parents around at the time. I very much doubt that they will wish to send their child to a school where pupils stick their teachers to chairs. Miss Fox was close to hysteria."

"We're ever so sorry," said Mrs Piff.

"I would like to think that Bobby was," said the Head. "However, he has some time to think about his conduct because I propose to bar him from school for the next two days. During which time I hope you will have a serious talk with him."

"We will," said Mr. Piff.

"Finally," said the Head, "I think it would be a good idea if I arranged for your son to be interviewed by the Educational Psychologist. He may be able to find out the causes of Bobby's bad behaviour. Would you agree?"

"We agree," they said.

Bobby only half listened to his parents' reproaches. Why had he done all these naughty things? Why didn't he try to be better? Why did he treat other people so badly?

"Don't know," he said to all these questions, but all the while he was thinking: two days off school! Brilliant! Shooting the Head by mistake hadn't got him any time off, but supergluing old Miss Fox on purpose got him two whole days! Why, he thought, if I can think up something really bad, I might get a week! And he went off into a daydream where he glued the Head and Miss Fox together and then used the pair of them for target practice with the patent Piff high-explosive imitation-blood bullet.

For Miss Fox, those two days seemed to flash by. If only he wasn't ever coming back, she thought, how much easier life would be for me. I'm the one who gets all the hassle – I expect that when he shot the Headmaster, he was really meaning to shoot me. And that glue! So embarrassing. And my skirt ruined. What will he do next? And why? Is it because he hates me? Perhaps the psychologist will find out. Perhaps it's me who needs the psychologist.

On the morning that Bobby returned to school, Miss Fox opened her register with a heavy heart.

Twice now she had been able to call out, "Bobby Piff?" knowing he wasn't there and couldn't reply.

Now she would read it and he would be there and wouldn't reply. But to her surprise he answered "Yes, Miss Fox," promptly, quietly, and politely, and when she looked up, even gave her that rather sweet smile.

In fact, Bobby was smiling to himself over a remarkable piece of luck he'd had that morning.

Before setting off for school he'd found a dead mouse in the garden and put it in his anorak pocket. What it had died of he didn't know, but it wasn't a bit chewed; it still looked as if it was alive.

Old Miss Fox is scared of spiders, he thought. Wonder what she's like with mice.

Shortly after Assembly that morning the Educational Psychologist arrived. A message came that Bobby Piff was to go to the Staff Room.

When he opened the door, Bobby found the Staff Room empty except for one rather strange figure, a tall thin man wearing blue jeans and a

fisherman's jersey, with sandals on his bare feet. He was quite bald, but he had a big bushy beard, so that Bobby thought his head looked upside down.

"Come along and sit down!" he said in a jolly voice.

Bobby came along and sat down.

"So you're Bobby Piff," said the bearded man.

Bobby nodded.

For some time the bearded man stared at him without speaking. Bobby stared back.

Funny looking old geezer, he said to himself, and he smiled.

Rather a sweet smile, thought the Educational Psychologist; the boy doesn't look like a trouble-maker. Perhaps there are problems at home.

"Now, Bobby," he said, "tell me a bit about yourself. Any brothers and sisters?"

Bobby shook his head.

"But you've got a mummy and a daddy."

"'Course," said Bobby. "Haven't you?"

"Ha, ha!" said the bearded man. An only child, he thought. Spoiled, perhaps.

"Your mummy and daddy spoil you, do they?"

he asked.

"No," said Bobby. "They've stopped my pocket money."

"But you like being at home, Bobby, do you? You're happiest there? You'd sooner be at home than at school?"

"'Course I would," said Bobby. What a thing to ask, he thought, he's a nutter, this one. Perhaps he's going to give me some more time off.

"So you don't like school?"

"Not much."

"Why is that?"

"They're always picking on me."

"Who, the other children?"

"No!" said Bobby scornfully. "They got more sense than to try. Anyone messes with me, they get a bunch of five."

"Who picks on you, then? The Headmaster?"

"Yes," said Bobby. "He stole my catapult."

"Confiscated it, d'you mean?"

"Stole it. It's mine and he's got it."

"What about your class teacher? What is she called?"

"Miss Fox."

"Don't you like her?"

"Not much."

"Why not?"

"She's always on at me."

"Why is that?"

"She doesn't like me, I s'pose."

The bearded man laced his fingers together and began to twiddle his thumbs, first one way, then the other. It was a nervous habit which he had been trying to cure himself of, but without success. It seemed to happen when he was thinking deeply.

This boy, he thought, lacks affection. Not at home perhaps, but at school he feels that every man's hand is against him. And every woman's. He needs a friend. He twiddled faster, while Bobby watched, fascinated.

"Bobby," he said at last. "*I* like you. Do you believe that?"

Bobby shook his head. He's a nutcase, he thought.

The Educational Psychologist stopped his twiddling and held out a hand.

"Bobby," he said. "I should like us to be friends. Will you shake hands?"

"OK," Bobby said.

"I shall see you again in a week's time," said the bearded man, "and don't forget – if there's anything I can do for you, just say. That's what friends are for."

"There is," Bobby said.

"What?"

"Get me my catapult back."

The bearded man thought, quickly. His thumbs twiddled again, even more quickly. I'll try to strike a bargain with him, he said to himself. No harm in that. He'll see me as an ally if I can do this for him.

"Now listen, Bobby," he said. "Do you think you can be a really good boy until I see you again?"

Bobby considered the likelihood of this. "Shouldn't think so," he said.

"Because if you can, then I'll do my best to persuade the Headmaster to allow you to have your catapult back."

Well, thought Bobby, he may be a bit of a

screwball, but it's worth a try.

"OK," he said.

As he made his way back to his classroom, the bell sounded, and the children came out to play. Bobby went to get his anorak. Not until he had put it on did he remember the dead mouse in its pocket. Then he went into the now empty classroom, took out the little corpse, and placed it, long tail outstretched, in the middle of his teacher's desk. It really did look alive.

But then he remembered what the man with the upside-down face had said.

He sighed.

Better not, he thought. Better wait until I get my catapult back. He looked around.

Just behind Miss Fox's desk was a wall radiator.

"Here," said Bobby to the mouse. "You'll keep nice and warm here," and he dropped it down behind.

Chapter 7

Cows on the Pitch

For Miss Fox the days that followed were like a miracle. It was as if chill winter had turned to glorious summer, as though brilliant sunshine had replaced dark clouds. Bobby Piff was behaving himself!

Not that he was helpful or co-operative – that would have been *too* much to expect – but at least he was no trouble in the classroom. Though Miss Fox was puzzled to find, when correcting his maths homework, that he had got almost every sum wrong. Bobby had been puzzled too, to find that the drawer where the Answer Book was kept had been locked. This, in fact, was because Miss Fox needed a safe place for the

Superglue.

After school on the day before the Educational Psychologist was next due, the Headmaster said to Miss Fox, "How has Bobby Piff been this week?"

"He's been no trouble at all," she replied. "I can't understand it."

"So you've had no problems?"

"Not with Bobby. There has been a most terrible smell in my classroom, right near to my desk, which at first I thought Bobby might have had something to do with. But the caretaker found that a poor little mouse had somehow got stuck behind the radiator and died."

No sooner had Bobby arrived at school next morning than he was summoned to the Headmaster's office, and the first thing he saw, on the desk, was his catapult.

The Head picked it up.

"Miss Fox tells me you've been behaving better," he said, "and high time, too."

And high time you gave me my catapult back, thought Bobby. Stealing it like that. You ought to be ashamed.

"I am going to give this back to you," said the Head.

Bobby held out a hand, smiling.

"After school."

The smile vanished.

"Can't I have it now?" said Bobby.

"No Bobby," said the Headmaster, "you cannot. You behave yourself for the rest of the day and then you can take it home and keep it there. You are never to bring it to school again. Understand?"

"OK," said Bobby.

"Yes, Sir."

"Yes . . . Sir."

After Assembly Bobby was again sent for, to go to the Staff Room, where he found the man with the upside-down face, who greeted him heartily.

"Sit down, Bobby, sit down," he said. "I'm so glad to hear that you've kept your nose clean and haven't blotted your copybook and haven't put a foot wrong and I think you should give yourself a pat on the back!"

What's he on about? thought Bobby. He's as

mad as a hatter, he is.

"And so now you're going to get your precious catapult back. You can thank me for that, you know. I persuaded the Headmaster. I told you, I'm your friend, remember?"

Bobby nodded. He sat looking at the Educational Psychologist, dressed today in a flowery shirt and bright red corduroy trousers and cowboy boots.

"You a teacher?" he said.

"No," said the bearded man. "Not in the way you mean. I'm a psychologist. Can you spell 'psychologist', Bobby my friend?"

"Spell it?" said Bobby. "I can't even say it. What's it mean?"

"It means that I study people's behaviour. I'm interested in what goes on in their minds."

"You're a mind-reader!"

"No, no, I wouldn't exactly say that."

"Read my mind," said Bobby. "Go on, have a go!" and he leaned forward and stared into the upside-down face, smiling at it. "I'm thinking about you," he said. "Tell me what I'm think-ing;" and he thought – what a funny-looking old chap you are, with your bald head and your bushy beard and the crazy things you say and all this stuff about us being friends, you ought to be in a lunatic asylum, you ought.

"Go on," he said. "Tell me."

The Educational Psychologist smiled back. Here's a chance, he said to himself, to do a little brainwashing.

"Well, Bobby," he said, " I guess – and it's only a guess – that you were thinking how much more pleasant school is if you can keep out of trouble and behave really well. You were thinking that now you've got me on your side, you're going to be really helpful and kind and nice to everyone from now on. Am I right?"

He's as nutty as a fruitcake, thought Bobby, but I'd better keep on the right side of him till I get my catapult back.

"Yes," he said. "You're right."

In fact Bobby had no intention of making a nuisance of himself for the rest of that day. He didn't answer Miss Fox back, he didn't make any rude noises in class, he didn't upset anyone in the playground, not even Kevin.

All might have been well if only temptation hadn't come his way, a temptation that Bobby simply couldn't resist.

It was football that afternoon for Bobby and the other boys of the two top classes, and there was a large number of spectators. They were all black-and-white – a herd of cows in the next-door field, that stood by the fence and watched in a bored sort of way.

Bobby's notion of footballing skill was always to go for the boy rather than the ball, and he flattened two or three opponents with over-enthusiastic tackles. The teacher refereeing the game was not best pleased.

"You watch it, Bobby," he said at half-time,

"or I'll be sending you off."

Bobby was not best pleased either.

There you are, he thought, picking on me as usual, and the second half had not long begun before he let off steam by tripping up an opposing forward and then punching him for good measure.

"Off, Bobby Piff!" shouted the referee, pointing an angry finger. "Go and stand on the touchline and stay there till I tell you."

"There you are," said Bobby as he stood watching the game go on without him. "No one else gets punished, only me," and from the other side of the fence came a sympathetic "Moo!"

Bobby looked round at the faces of the black-and-white spectators, and it was then that temptation reared its ugly head.

A little way up the fence was a gate. Bobby edged his way along the touchline till he was near it.

No one noticed, neither teacher nor boys. All were too intent on the game of football.

Bobby opened the gate.

No one noticed. No one, that is, except the

cows, who decided, after a little while, that the grass on the other side of the fence would be greener.

First one made her way through the gateway, then two or three together, and then the whole herd came shoving and pushing through.

Wild with excitement at the thrill of escape, fifty great galumphing Friesians went charging across the football pitch, leaping and kicking and bawling and buckjumping as though they were young again, while the referee and twenty-one footballers fled in all directions, and the twenty-second watched happily.

Later, after an angry farmer had come to collect his cattle from a pitch now peppered with cowpats, and an angry teacher had reported the whole matter, Bobby Piff stood before a very angry Headmaster.

"How did that gate come to be open?" said the Head.

"It swung open," said Bobby, truthfully.

It had. He'd swung it.

"Did you deliberately open that gate and let those cows in to the playing field? Yes or no."

"Yes," said Bobby, honestly.

"Do you realise the damage you have caused?

The football pitch is in a disgusting mess, one of the goalposts is broken, the teacher who was refereeing has twisted his ankle in trying to dodge the cows, and one of them trod on the football and burst it. And you aren't even sorry, are you?"

"No," said Bobby, honestly.

"Last time I suspended you from school, Bobby," said the Headmaster, "it was for two days. This time it will be for three."

Great, thought Bobby, I'll be getting a whole week off before long.

It was then that almost everybody in the school heard, coming from the Headmaster's office, a deafening bellow of "NO!"

Whatever's happening? they thought.

They did not know that Bobby Piff had just said, "Now can I have my catapult back?"

Chapter 8

Ten out of Ten

"To call Bobby Piff a pain in the neck," said the Headmaster, "is to make light of the matter. There are degrees of pain, and this is becoming agony."

"If only I could interest him more in his work," said Miss Fox. "His maths did improve greatly, but now it's suddenly got worse again."

"Affection," said the Educational Psychologist. "Affection and understanding, that's what the boy wants. I offered myself as a friend and I think he was beginning to appreciate that. Friendship, that's what I think he needs."

"I know what I think he needs," said the Headmaster, "but unfortunately I'm not allowed to use it."

"Corporal punishment, do you mean?" asked the Educational Psychologist in horrified tones. "Oh no, you cannot be serious?"

"Deadly," said the Head.

"Perhaps," said Miss Fox, "the fault lies with me. Perhaps I am too harsh with Bobby."

"Impossible," said the Head.

"Miss Fox has a point," said the Educational Psychologist. "Boys like that sometimes react well to being encouraged. The carrot, you know, not the stick. Perhaps Bobby could be given special responsibilities in the classroom . . ."

"As long as it's not putting out the paints," said the Head.

" . . . so that he feels that he's being a help to Miss Fox, that she is relying on him. It will make him feel that he is being singled out, that he is different from all the other children."

"He is," said the Head.

"I'll certainly try," said Miss Fox.

"Oh, good show!" said the Educational Psychologist, gushingly.

"And good luck," said the Headmaster, drily.

Thus it was that when Bobby returned at the end of his three-day suspension, he was greeted by a smiling Miss Fox, who said she was glad to see him back. She had managed the smile, and the lie, rather well, she told herself.

"We've missed you, Bobby," she said, and the rest of the class looked at her in astonishment.

Bobby also was surprised. She's taking the mickey, he thought, she'd better watch out.

After Assembly, Miss Fox said, "Now then, children, this morning we're going to try something a little bit different. We're going to try some descriptive writing."

She picked up the pile of newly-corrected exercise books on her desk and said "Bobby Piff, will you give these out, please?"

What's up with her? Bobby thought. She's never let me do that again since I frisbied them all across the classroom and hit some stupid girl on the nose and made her cry. Puzzled, he gave out the books sensibly, as any ordinary child would have done.

"Right," said Miss Fox. "Now then, when we look at people, we mostly don't look carefully enough to be able to describe them accurately. We just notice obvious things about them, like whether they're fair or dark, or tall or short, or thin . . ."

" . . . or thick," said Bobby.

Miss Fox gave a light laugh. "But," she went on, "we seldom really study someone thoughtfully, so that we can give a complete and true description. Now this morning I want you to choose some other person in this class and write a description of him or her. Perhaps it will be the boy or girl sitting opposite you at your table, because he or she will be the easiest for you to look at. Try to notice not just the colour of eyes or hair, but everything about the person. You must say who it is you are describing, of course, and then I can judge how well you've done it. For example, Bobby is sitting opposite Kevin, so he might choose to describe him. He'll look carefully at him, not just his face but the whole of him, and then say what he looks like."

"A rat," said Bobby.

Miss Fox managed another little laugh. "You're joking, of course, Bobby," she said.

"Now then, everyone decide on your subject, and think carefully, and we'll see who is really observant."

"Can we choose anybody?" said Bobby.

"Anybody in the classroom," said Miss Fox. "Anyone you like."

Don't know about liking, thought Bobby, but I know who I'm choosing.

For a while there was quiet in the room, the sort of quiet that only usually occurred in Bobby Piff's absence. But he, Miss Fox noticed, seemed to be both writing and thinking deeply. Several times she caught him looking at her, perhaps for inspiration, she thought, and she smiled at him encouragingly.

Now and again a child would ask how to spell a word, and then the teacher would write it on the blackboard.

"Please, Miss," said a giggling girl, "how d'you spell 'handsome'?" and a boy wanted to know if 'pigtail' was one word or two.

Bobby put up a hand to ask for the spelling of 'spectacles', and Miss Fox looked with relief at the only child in the class who wore them, a red-haired boy sitting near Bobby. At least he's not writing about Kevin, she thought.

"Now don't forget," she said when everyone had finished, "to put the person's name at the top of your description. And Bobby – perhaps you would collect the books up for me?"

"Yes, Miss Fox," said Bobby with a smile.

"Good boy," said Miss Fox. Miracles do happen, she thought. Don't they?

Once again Bobby collected the books in what seemed a sensible manner. True, there was a sudden squawk from Kevin and a cry of "He trod on my foot!" but Bobby said, "Sorry, Kevin, I never seen it."

"You never *saw* it," said Miss Fox.

"That's right."

During the midday break Miss Fox sat in the Staff Room, eating her lunch and correcting the descriptions. Some people, when they eat, save the best bits till last. Some eat them first and leave what they don't much like till the end. Miss Fox put Bobby Piff's story-book at the bottom of the pile.

Most of the descriptions, she was relieved to find, were fairly inoffensive. No one had used the word 'ugly', and a fat child was politely referred to as 'plump'.

Let's just hope, she thought, as she came at last to Bobby's book, that he hasn't been too cruel about the red-haired boy with spectacles.

She opened the book, and there, she saw with horror, was her own name.

Miss Fox.

My teacher is called Miss Fox and she is quite old. I dont no how old because her hair is quite black with no grey hairs but I think she dies it. It sticks out all round her face like a mop but I dont no if it grows like that or if she never comes it. I can't see what couler her eyes are because she wears spectacles. She has a long nose and her teeth are too big. Her face is pale and she has lines on her forred. She is tall and thin and she wears funny dresses, not trowsers like some other womin teachers. She has big feet. She is fritened of spiders.

Miss Fox closed the book. All true, she thought, all true, as a tear ran down her long nose. If only he could have said a kind word.

All through the afternoon's teaching she thought of Bobby Piff's description of her. It had hurt, as he had meant it to, she supposed. But he had done what she had asked. 'Notice everything about the person', she had said, and he had. He deserved good marks. But how the other children would laugh when he showed them what he'd written, because he'd show them all right, no doubt about that.

When the bell rang for the end of school and Miss Fox had dismissed the class, she nerved herself to say, "Bobby, would you stay behind a minute?"

"OK," said Bobby.

When the others had gone, Miss Fox opened Bobby's story-book and showed it to him.

Under his description she had written:

Well done, Bobby. $\dfrac{10}{10}$

Bobby looked. They're all going mad around here, he thought. First there's that crazy guy with the upside-down face and now old Foxy's at it. She's given me full marks!

"You've given me full marks," he said.

"Yes," said Miss Fox, "you described me very well indeed," and Bobby was close enough to see that, behind the spectacles, her eyes were not only brown but also full of tears.

"I wasn't trying to be rude," he said. "You said 'notice everything' and I did."

Miss Fox blew her long nose. "Yes, you did," she said. "I asked for it and I got it. I'm very pleased that you took trouble with this, Bobby,

that's why I took no notice of a few mistakes in spelling or punctuation, or the handwriting, and gave you ten out of ten. But I would like to ask you a favour."

"What's that?"

"I don't really want you showing this to your special friends."

"Haven't got any special friends," said Bobby.

"I mean . . . I'd be happier if you didn't show it to anyone."

Bobby looked at his teacher, puzzled. Funny old thing, he thought, she's in a proper stew about something.

"They all know you're scared of spiders," he said.

"Yes, I don't mean just that bit."

"They all know what you look like."

"Yes. All the same, I'd rather we kept this to ourselves."

"Just you and me?" said Bobby.

"Just you and me."

"OK," said Bobby, "you can rely on me. Can I go now?"

"Yes, of course. And thank you, Bobby."

"That's all right," said Bobby. At the classroom door he stopped and turned and smiled.

"See you," he said.

"See you," said Miss Fox, smiling back.

Chapter 9

Clint's Ear

"Guess what," said Bobby to his mother later. "I got full marks for some writing today. Old Foxy gave me ten out of ten."

"Oh, Bobby!" said Mrs Piff. "That *is* nice! But I don't think you ought to speak about Miss Fox like that."

"Why not?"

"It's not respectful."

Bobby did not reply to this. For one thing, he wasn't sure what 'respectful' meant. For another, he didn't care.

"You like Miss Fox, don't you?" asked his mother.

Bobby considered this. The man with the

upside-down face had asked him the same question, and he'd said, "Not much". But old Foxy hadn't been too bad today. She hadn't picked on him, she'd let him give out the books and collect them, and she'd given him full marks. No one had ever done that before.

"She's all right," he said.

Wonder if she could get my catapult back for me, he thought. The Headmaster won't let me have it, and that psycho-whatsit chap, he said he'd get it for me but he never did. Maybe old Foxy could, if I keep on the right side of her. I'll try it.

Next morning, to Miss Fox's surprise, Bobby Piff was the first child to arrive. Normally he slouched in last, looking stony-faced, and usually proceeded to upset any children unlucky enough to be sitting near him by kicking them under the table, or jogging their arms as they tried to write or draw, or turning their reading books upside down so that the markers fell out.

Now he came in with a smile – and Miss Fox thought again what a nice smile it was – and said "Hello!"

"Oh hello, Bobby," said Miss Fox.

"Nice day, isn't it?" said Bobby.

Miss Fox looked out of the classroom window at a number of children and parents dashing across the playground through the pouring rain.

"Well . . . " she said doubtfully.

"Anything I can do?" said Bobby, coming up to her desk and standing before it. "Sharpen your pencils?"

"Well," said Miss Fox. "I think . . ."

"Clean the blackboard?"

"Well, no, Bobby, thank you, I've just written a lot of sums on it."

"Tell you what," said Bobby. "I'll have a look in the stock cupboard. See if there's any old spiders in there."

"Well, yes, but . . ."

"Soon get rid of 'em for you. Don't worry, I won't show 'em to you, I'll put 'em outside," said Bobby.

The fact that he could not find a spider in the stock cupboard did not deter Bobby. He pretended that he had. After a while he came out with his hands cupped together, as he had once before. He gave Miss Fox a reassuring wink and went out of the classroom as the other children were coming in.

"Miss! Miss! I just saw Bobby Piff going out!" said Kevin. "He had something in his hands."

"Yes, I know," said Miss Fox. "He's just getting rid of something for me."

"What, Miss?"

"Never you mind."

"Where's he going, then?"

"Outside."

"But it's raining."

"Sit down, Kevin," said Miss Fox.

What a little telltale he is, she thought, I'd sooner have Bobby with all his faults.

Bobby had in fact been struck by an idea. All the children had by now gone into their classrooms and there was no one in the main corridor. Bobby hurried down it towards the Headmaster's office. I'll just have a peep, he thought, in case the door's open, and if he's not there, well, I'll just nip in and see if that drawer's unlocked and get my catapult. That's not stealing, you can't steal your own stuff.

In fact the door of the office was open and the Headmaster was not there, and Bobby was inside and actually reaching for the handle of the drawer when he heard heavy footsteps.

He straightened up and stood smartly to attention beside the desk.

"What are you doing here?" said the Head.

"Please, sir," said Bobby, "Miss Fox sent me to see you."

The Head's face darkened. "Bobby Piff!" he said. "I am fed up to the back teeth with you. Never a day passes, never an hour, never a minute, it seems sometimes, that you aren't making a nuisance of yourself in one way or another. Can you wonder that people get angry with you? What have you been doing wrong now, you wretched boy, you?"

"Please, sir," said Bobby. "Nothing."

"Then why has Miss Fox sent you to me?"

"To tell you that she gave me full marks for my writing yesterday. She gave me ten out of ten. She said she was very pleased with me, sir."

"Good heavens!" said the Headmaster. "It seems I owe you an apology, Bobby."

"That's OK," said Bobby, smiling.

For a moment the psychologist's words came into the Head's mind. "Affection and understanding. That's what the boy wants." I can't understand him, and as for affection, well, that's asking a lot. But maybe I should give him his blasted catapult back.

"Come and see me at the end of school, Bobby," he said.

"Wherever have you been, Bob[...] Miss Fox on his return.

"The Headmaster asked me to do son[...] said Bobby truthfully.

At morning break the Head said to Miss Fox, "Bobby Piff tells me that you gave him ten out of ten yesterday."

"He told you that, did he?"

"Yes. Why, is it not true?"

"Oh, yes. He did a good piece of work."

"Splendid. You must show it to me some-time."

"Well, er . . ."

"And he's behaving well in class?"

"Yes. At the moment."

"Good, good," said the Head. Could this leopard be changing his spots? he thought. He called me 'Sir' three times this morning without being told.

By midday the rain had stopped and the sun was shining, and after lunch the children all went out into the playground. Miss Fox, return-ing to her classroom, found Bobby there, alone, moving around the room, wastepaper bin in

"Why aren't you outside?" she said.

"Tidying up," said Bobby. "Messy lot of kids we got in here," and he picked up some more bits of paper from the floor.

"Well, that's kind of you, Bobby," said Miss Fox, "but I don't want you missing your playtime. Off you go now, there's a good boy."

There's a good boy, she thought – fancy saying that about Bobby Piff! Long may it last.

But alas, it didn't.

All would have been well if Miss Fox had only chosen a different story to read to the class at the end of the day.

"This story," she said when they were all comfortably settled on the floor in the book corner, "is about a fox. Before I start, let me ask you all – who has ever seen a fox?"

Some hands went up.

"I saw one in the field behind our house once," said someone.

"I saw one that had been run over," said another.

"I've seen them on the telly," said several others.

"I seen you, Miss," said Bobby.

Miss Fox laughed. "I meant the four-legged kind, Bobby," she said, and she began to read the story.

When she had finished, she closed the book and said, "If I asked you to describe a fox in one word, what would you say?"

'Clever' and 'intelligent', 'sly' and 'cunning' were some of the suggestions, but one child said 'beautiful', and the teacher said, "Yes, I think we'd all agree that foxes are beautiful animals."

All might still have been well if Bobby had not happened to be sitting next to a big fat boy called Clint.

"Foxes aren't all beautiful," whispered Clint to Bobby, grinning. "The one in this classroom is really ugly."

The next moment he gave a loud yell of pain as Bobby grabbed hold of his ear and twisted it as hard as he could.

"What is going on?" cried Miss Fox.

"Oh, my ear!" howled Clint. "He's nearly pulled it off!"

"Who did?"

"Bobby Piff!" cried everyone.

"Bobby, why did you do that?"

"Because of what he said."

"What did he say?"

Bobby did not answer. I can't tell her that, he thought. It's not that I mind about getting that stupid fat Clint into trouble. I just can't tell her that he said she was ugly, not in front of everyone.

"Well?" said Miss Fox.

"Oh, nothing," said Bobby.

"Right," said Miss Fox. "You will stay behind when the class is dismissed."

"Come in!" called the Headmaster in answer to a knock on the door of his office a little later, and in came Miss Fox and Bobby Piff.

"Ah yes, Bobby," said the Head. "I told you to come and see me, didn't I?" and he opened the drawer and took out the catapult. "Miss Fox tells me you've been behaving much better lately," he said, "and so I have decided–"

"Just a moment, please," said Miss Fox hurriedly. "I'm afraid I have to tell you that Bobby has just savagely attacked a boy in my class. For no reason at all that I can discover."

There was a short silence.

Then, slowly, the Headmaster put the catapult back into the drawer with one hand, while with the other he rubbed the back of his neck, as though he had a pain in it.

"This," he said, "is the limit."

Chapter 10

Extra Strong Mints

"Who was this boy that Bobby attacked?" asked the Headmaster.

"It was Clint," said Miss Fox. "I asked Bobby why, and he told me it was because of something that Clint said, but he wouldn't tell me what it was."

"It was rude," said Bobby. "That's why."

"Miss Fox," said the Head, "would you go and find Mrs Piff – she may be waiting for Bobby – and tell her he'll be along shortly?"

"Now Bobby," he went on once she had gone, "are you going to tell me what Clint said?"

"If you don't tell Miss Fox."

"Whatever d'you mean, boy? Are you saying

he used bad language?"

"No."

"What, then?"

"He was rude about Miss Fox. He said a nasty thing about her, so I twisted his ear."

What next? thought the Head. Wonders will never cease! Bobby Piff standing up for his teacher.

"What was this nasty thing that Clint said about Miss Fox?" he asked.

"Well, he said she was ugly. We were talking about foxes and someone said they were beautiful and Clint said the one in our class was really ugly."

"I see," said the Head slowly. "And that made you angry?"

"Yes."

Dear, oh dear, thought the Head – no one could say that Muriel Fox was a beauty, that's true enough, but fancy Bobby Piff handing out rough justice on her behalf – and once again he recalled the psychologist's words about affection and understanding. Perhaps she was getting through to the boy. Perhaps some change was taking place. The old Bobby would simply have agreed with Clint or added something ruder still about Miss Fox. The new one, if it was a new one, had stood up for her. Still, he could not go unpunished. He took out his pen and pulled a sheet of paper towards him.

Bobby stood waiting. He won't give me my catapult now, he thought, but I might get some more days off school. What's he writing? Can't read it upside down.

The Headmaster thrust the paper at him. "What does that say?" he asked.

"I must not take the law into my own hands," read Bobby.

"Do you understand what that means?"

No, thought Bobby. "Yes," he said.

"Copy it out one hundred times – in your best handwriting – and bring it to me this time to-morrow. Now go."

Next day Bobby arrived in the classroom even earlier, long before any other children.

Why had he been so good and helpful yesterday, thought Miss Fox, and then spoiled it all by attacking Clint like that?

"Please," Bobby said, "can I have some paper? I got to do a hundred lines for Sir. I can get some done now, before lessons, and then can I stay in at break and do some more, please? And at lunchtime, if I haven't finished?"

"We'll see," said Miss Fox, giving him the paper.

"Before the other children arrive, Bobby," she said, "will you tell me now exactly what it was that Clint said to you yesterday?"

"I don't want to," said Bobby.

"You said it was rude. Was he being rude about you?"

"About me? Oh yes, yes, he was. He called me a rude name."

"I see," said Miss Fox. "Still, you know, you mustn't take the law into your own hands."

Bobby smiled at her. "Funny you should say that," he said.

When the class was dismissed at the end of school, Bobby set off to the Headmaster's office with his hundred lines. Once again, he had made a change here and there to relieve the boredom, by writing

> 'I must not take the lav into my own hands'.

If he notices, he thought, I'll say "No, that's not a *v*, that's a *w* gone a bit wrong."

He knocked on the office door, but there was no answering call to enter.

Bobby opened the door and went in and put his lines on the desk. Then he paused. He could just imagine his poor old catapult crying out to be rescued from its dark prison, and once again he reached out and this time actually took hold of the handle of the drawer. Then something made him look round.

Miss Fox was standing in the doorway, watching.

They stared at one another.

Then, slowly and deliberately, Miss Fox shook her head.

"Bobby," she said, "I think you'd better be off. Your mum will be waiting."

"Yes, Miss Fox," replied Bobby. He smiled as he passed her.

"Thanks, Miss Fox," he said.

Before long the Educational Psychologist paid another visit, dressed this time in a purple tracksuit and orange trainers. By the time he sent for Bobby he had heard from the Headmaster all about the incident of Clint's ear.

"Standing up for his teacher, was he?" he said. "That's very promising. I'll work on that," and when Bobby arrived in the Staff Room, he lost no time in bringing the subject up.

"Well, Bobby my friend," he said, shaking hands, "I hear you've been doing really well since I saw you last. Getting full marks for some of your work, they tell me."

Bobby nodded.

The bearded man laced his fingers together and began to twiddle his thumbs, first one way, then the other.

"But," he said, "I understand you've been in a spot of trouble, too. Something to do with a boy called Clint? He said something rude about Miss Fox? In fact, he said she was ugly?"

Bobby nodded again.

"Tell me, Bobby," said the bearded man, twiddling like mad, "do *you* think Miss Fox is ugly?"

Yes, thought Bobby. "No," he said.

He began to feel angry. It's none of your business what I think, he said to himself. Old Foxy's a beauty queen compared to you with your upside-down face and your stupid clothes. You're a weirdo, you are.

"Can I go now?" he said.

The Educational Psychologist stopped twiddling and stood up. I shouldn't have asked that, he thought.

"You like Miss Fox now, don't you?" he said.
"No," said Bobby. Yes, he thought.

At break time he went out into the playground still feeling angry – with the psycho-whatsit for being so nosy, with the Head for hanging on to his catapult, with that stupid fat Clint for being stupid and fat.

It was Clint's bad luck to be in Bobby's way as he strode, scowling, through the playground. As always, the noise of shouting children running, jumping and skipping about was deafening, and no-one particularly noticed another loud yell from Clint, as Bobby Piff got hold of his other ear and gave it a good twisting. Nor did anyone

else hear Bobby say, "And if you tell on me to old Foxy, I'll pull both your ears right off."

For the rest of that morning Bobby was a menace in class. He talked when supposed to be silent, fidgeted when meant to be still, doodled instead of writing, upset his neighbours in one way or another, and generally made Miss Fox's life a misery.

To her cries of "Who did that?" "Who said that?" "Who was that?" came always the same answer – "*Bobby Piff!*"

He was so much better the other day, she thought, but now he's his old self again. Why is he being so bad today? At lunchtime she sent for him.

"Sit down, Bobby," she said. "You have been a perfect nuisance this morning. Tell me what the matter is."

"Nothing," said Bobby.

"Was it something the psychologist said to you?"

"Something he asked me," said Bobby. "He's nosy, he is. And he's the one that said he'd get me my catapult back but he never done it."

"He never *did* it," said Miss Fox.

"No, he never."

"What was it that he asked you?"

"Can't tell you."

Miss Fox sighed. "Well, if you can't tell me what's troubling you, Bobby," she said, "I can't help you."

"Don't need any help," said Bobby.

"Don't you?" said Miss Fox wearily. She took off her spectacles and began to polish them.

"Most of us do," she said. "I was very glad of your help the other day. 'You can rely on me', you said, I remember. I should like to think that I still can."

Because she was, for once, without her spectacles, Bobby noticed how tired her eyes looked, and he suddenly began to feel unhappy with himself. Poor old Foxy, he thought. I wish I'd never written that stuff about her. She's not really ugly, she's got a nice face. He wanted to say he was sorry for behaving badly but he couldn't make himself.

He put his hand in his pocket and pulled out the remains of a tube of Extra Strong Mints.

There were only two left in it, and the outside one looked distinctly grubby, more grey than white.

"Have a mint," he said.

Miss Fox put on her spectacles and examined the offering doubtfully.

"You haven't got many left," she said.

"There's one for each of us," said Bobby, and he put the grey mint in his mouth and held out the last, still-white one. Miss Fox took it.

"Thank you, Bobby," she said, popping it between her large teeth.

"That's OK," said Bobby. "They're extra strong, mind."

"My favourites," lied Miss Fox gallantly.

But she could not deceive herself about how pleased she felt when, next morning, Bobby Piff again arrived first and plonked a new, full, untouched tube of Extra Strong Mints in front of her.

"Present for you," he said. "Only don't tell no one."

"I won't tell *any*one," said Miss Fox.

Chapter 11

A Broken Wrist

"Bobby Piff is making progress, wouldn't you say?" asked the Educational Psychologist on his next visit.

"No," said the Head.

"Yes," said Miss Fox. "He's been much less trouble recently."

"Good, good!" said the Educational Psychologist. "Don't you think, Headmaster, that now he might have his catapult back?"

"No," said the Head.

"Perhaps I could have it?" said Miss Fox.

"Why, Muriel!" said the Head. "I didn't know you were a keen catapultier?"

"No, no," said Miss Fox. "I just thought that

maybe you could leave it to me to decide when Bobby deserves to have it back."

"Oh, very well," said the Headmaster. He took out the catapult and handed it to her. "I'm sick of the sight of the thing," he said, "always reminding me of the boy. But I should keep it under lock and key if I were you – I wouldn't put it past Master Piff to steal it if he got the chance."

"Oh, I don't think he'd do such a thing," said Miss Fox.

A day or so later all the children in the school were told at Assembly that there was to be a fire drill that morning. The fire alarm would ring, and then each class must follow its teacher out into the playground and stand quietly in line while a roll-call was taken.

"And shut all doors behind you," the Headmaster said. "Teachers, will you each please choose one boy or girl in your class to be responsible for shutting your classroom door as you leave."

Normally Miss Fox would have chosen a sensible girl, or almost any boy except Bobby Piff, but, back in her classroom, she said, "Now when the alarm goes, you will come out last, Bobby, and shut the door behind you. Understand?"

"Yes, Miss Fox," said Bobby.

And quite soon the fire alarm did go off.

"Line up, children, quickly and quietly," said Miss Fox, "and Bobby, don't forget what you've got to do."

"No, Miss Fox," said Bobby.

It was only after he had shut the classroom door and was about to follow the rest down the corridor that two things occurred to him. One, he would pass the Headmaster's office, last of everybody. Two, the whole school, including the Head, would be outside in the playground. There would be no one at all left inside.

I needn't knock, he thought, I'll just open the door, and nip in, and get it, and out again. First it was the Head that caught me and then old Foxy, but this time there's no one to catch me, it'll be third time lucky.

He dawdled until the others had gone out into the playground, and then he whipped into the office and opened the drawer.

There was no catapult in it!

Quickly he tried the other drawers. No sign of it.

Out he went again, shutting the door behind him, but by the time he neared the main doors that led out to the playground, he could see that all the classes were already lined up on the far side, and that the Headmaster was going from one to another, checking that everyone had answered their names.

"All present, Miss Fox?" he asked when he reached her.

"No," said Miss Fox, "there's a boy missing."

They looked at one another.

"Is it . . . ?" said the Head.

"Yes," said Miss Fox.

Angrily the Head strode back towards the main entrance.

Peeping through the window, Bobby saw him coming, and was suddenly struck by a brilliant idea.

I'll fool him, he thought, I'll pretend I fell down and hurt myself and that's why I'm late.

An ordinary boy – if an ordinary boy would have thought of such a crackbrained scheme – would just have lain down on the floor of the corridor and arranged himself to look as though he had had a fall, but Bobby was never one to do things by halves. Remembering a scene from a video where the baddie had been hit by a hail of bullets and had leaped dramatically in the air before crashing to the ground, dead, he leaped and crashed.

The Headmaster opened the double doors to find Bobby Piff lying on the floor, groaning loudly. What's he up to now? he thought.

"What have you done?" he said.

"Oh, my wrist, my wrist!" cried Bobby. "Oh, it hurts something awful!"

"At first I thought he was just pretending," said the Headmaster to the rest of the staff at lunchtime. "You all know what Bobby Piff is like. I thought he was putting it all on, as an excuse for having been absent from fire drill. But in fact he has broken a bone – the hospital just phoned to give me the result of the X-ray. He may be a pain in the neck, but now he's got a pain in his wrist."

"Poor Bobby!" said Miss Fox. "Will he be kept in?"

"No, no, they'll put it in plaster and send him home. He'll be back at school tomorrow."

When he arrived, Bobby seemed remarkably cheerful.

"Look," he said, thrusting his right arm at her, plastered from elbow to fingertips. "Look what they done to me."

"*Did* to you," said Miss Fox automatically. "You'll be able to get all the class to sign their names on it, won't you?"

"Don't want their rotten old names," said Bobby. "I just want yours. Can I have your autograph, please?"

"Of course you can," said Miss Fox, and with a red felt pen she wrote *Muriel J. Fox* on the white plaster.

Bobby examined this.

"Really," he said, "you ought to put 'Best Wishes'. People do." So she did.

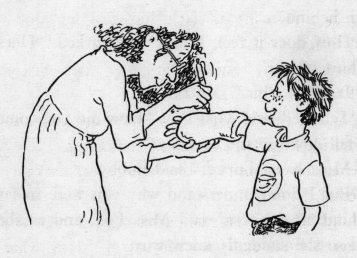

Watching her, Bobby said with great satisfaction, "Shan't be able to write anything, you know."

"Goodness!" said Miss Fox. "Nor will you. Still, you can read, and there's no reason you can't do some maths. Anyone can write figures with their left hand."

Later Bobby was allowed to go all round the class, so that every boy and girl could write their names on his plaster.

"And don't you go writing anything nasty," he said softly to Clint, "or you know what'll happen."

When the bell went for lunch, Miss Fox kept him behind.

"How does it feel, Bobby?" she asked. "Does it hurt much?"

"It aches a bit," said Bobby.

"Tell me," said Miss Fox. "How did you come to fall down in the corridor?"

"Must have slipped," said Bobby.

"But I don't understand why you were so far behind all the rest,' said Miss Fox, and as she did so she suddenly knew why.

"Bobby," she said. "Don't tell me you went into the Headmaster's office again?"

Bobby looked at his teacher, with her fuzzy hair and her long nose and her big teeth, and decided he could not lie to her.

"Yes, I did," he said.

"To get your catapult."

"Yes. But it wasn't there."

"I know," said Miss Fox. "I've got it."

Bobby smiled that nice smile of his.

"Oh, if you've got it," he said, "that's all right, then. You'll give it back to me one of these days, I know. I can rely on you."

Chapter 12

The Rescue

To her surprise and pleasure, Miss Fox found that Bobby in plaster was far better behaved than normal. This may have been partly due to the fact that he was unable to hit anyone with his right hand, should he so have wished. But because he couldn't write with it either, Miss Fox had to treat him rather differently from the other children, and this Bobby obviously liked.

He even made brave efforts to try writing with his left hand, though these were not very successful: Bobby's handwriting at best was not good, but left-handed it was a mystery.

However figures, as Miss Fox had said, were

easier to do, and she gave him a lot of sums, at times when the rest of the class were doing other things.

"When you've finished these," she said to him one morning, "you can correct them yourself."

"How am I going to know if they're right?" asked Bobby.

"I'll give you my Answer Book, and you can put a tick or a cross against each sum. With a red pen, just in case you're tempted to alter any that are wrong."

"Who, me?" said Bobby with a look of amazement.

Later, he came to stand beside her desk.

"I've finished, Miss," he said, "but I don't know where the Answer Book is kept."

"No, you wouldn't," said Miss Fox.

She unlocked the drawer, in which, Bobby could see, was not only the Answer Book but also the Superglue, the catapult, and the tube of Extra Strong Mints he had given her.

Quietly, so that the rest couldn't hear, he said, "You haven't eaten any of your mints."

"Saving them up," said Miss Fox equally quietly, "for a treat." But giving Bobby the Answer Book, she discovered, was not a good idea. When she came to look at his work later, she found he had marked each and every sum as correct. He must have altered some of them, she thought, but she could not see that any of the figures had been changed. She checked the answers. Half of them were wrong, but that hadn't deterred Bobby from putting a large red tick against them all.

Another result of Bobby's injury was that he couldn't play games or do PE, so that at these times Miss Fox had to find other things to occupy him. Once or twice she took her class to the hall, leaving him in the classroom with his reading book. She arranged for the teacher in the next door room to look in on him at regular intervals.

"I don't think he'll be any trouble," she said.

I hope not, anyway, she thought.

And he wasn't. The other teacher only saw

Bobby Piff bent over his reading book, and knew nothing of the pile of comics on his lap beneath the table.

Soon it was half-term, a time that to Miss Fox had meant one thing above all others: for a whole week she would be free of Bobby Piff. But this time it felt somehow different.

And instead of dreading the start of the second half of the term (because of the old Bobby), she actually found herself quite looking forward to it (because of the new Bobby).

Her feelings were not shared among the children of the class. To them Bobby Piff was what he had always been – someone looking for trouble and usually finding it, someone to be wary of (specially if you were Kevin or Clint), someone without a friend. They did not realise that now he had one.

On the first day of the second half of term there began such a spell of wet weather as no one could remember.

All Tuesday it rained too, and Wednesday, and Thursday, and by the evening of that day there were flood alert warnings everywhere and pictures on TV of wretched people mopping out their water-logged homes.

A stream ran beside the road down which most of the children came to school, a little brook that was normally no more than a few metres wide and a metre or so deep. But now it had turned into a rushing river, and those that threw sticks into it as they walked down the road saw them whisked away on the brown torrent.

On the Friday morning Miss Fox sat in her empty classroom, looking out of the window at the never-ending rain, and waiting for the children to arrive. She found herself hoping that Bobby would be first in, with his now usual cheery greeting, but he wasn't. Instead, half a dozen boys and girls burst in excitedly, all talking at once.

"Miss Fox! Miss Fox!" they cried. "Bobby's in the brook! He was fighting with Samantha and he fell in!" Samantha was the big quick-tempered eleven-year-old girl with whom Bobby had tangled in the past.

The first thought that flashed into Miss Fox's mind was that Bobby could swim. She knew this from giving swimming lessons in the local baths. The second thought was that he couldn't, not with one arm encased in a heavy plaster.

She leaped to her feet and ran out of the classroom.

Across the playground she dashed through the teeming rain and on to the road, where she could see a huddle of figures moving anxiously along the bank of the flooded brook.

Everyone was shouting or screaming, but no-one among the children or various parents seemed to be doing anything much to help, except for the lollipop lady: she was trying to reach out with her long standard to the figure

that was being swept along by the current.

Miss Fox, coatless, drenched, her fuzzy hair now hanging in rats' tails, could see in the brown water the whiteness of Bobby's plastered arm and of his frightened face, as he tried desperately to keep afloat. "Oh give us a hand, someone!" cried Bobby Piff, and with a shout of "Coming Bobby!", into the rushing torrent plunged Miss Muriel Fox.

Chapter 13

Good Old Foxy

O n the following Monday morning Miss Fox sat at her desk as usual, marking books and waiting for the children to arrive.

Since the drama of Bobby's rescue she had been besieged by admiring people. Mr and Mrs Piff had, of course, been profuse in their thanks and gratitude; everyone on the staff had praised her, all the children regarded her as a heroine, and the local newspaper had put the story on its front page, including an old and none too flattering photograph of her.

The only person, it seemed, that she had not seen was Bobby, who had been taken away in an ambulance on that Friday morning.

Will he come to school today, she wondered?

In answer to this unspoken question the door opened and there stood Bobby Piff.

"Hello," he said, smiling.

He walked, awkwardly, across the room to the teacher's desk and stuck out his right hand.

"Thanks," he said in a gruff voice.

"That's all right," said Miss Fox, and she stretched out her hand and shook his, and then she realised.

"Oh, Bobby!" she said. "You've had your plaster removed!"

"Yes," Bobby said. "Mind you," he said, "I probably won't be able to do much writing for a bit. The wrist's sure to ache if I do."

"Of course," said Miss Fox.

She took out the catapult from the drawer of her desk. "You probably won't be able to use this yet, either," she said.

"I dunno about that," said Bobby. "But it'd be nice to have it back."

Good old Foxy, he thought.

"Here it is, then," said Miss Fox. "And by the way, tell me – how did you come to fall in the

brook the other day? Did someone push you?"

"No," said Bobby.

"What happened, then?"

"If I tell you," said Bobby, "you won't tell no one else?"

"I won't tell anyone else," said Miss Fox.

"Well, you see," said Bobby, "I got mad at that old Samantha and I was trying to push her in."

Bad, bad Bobby, thought Miss Fox.

"But she's heavy, see, and I must of lost my balance and I fell in. Good job you come along."

"Good job I *came* along."

Bobby Piff smiled his sweet smile. "Yes, Miss Fox," he said.

YOUNG HIPPO MAGIC

Anything is possible in these enchanting stories
from Young Hippo Magic!

My Friend's a Gris-Quok
Malorie Blackman

Alex has a deep, dark secret. He's half Gris-Quok!

The Little Pet Dragon
Philippa Gregory

James' puppy dog is glimmering with a very strong
magic!

Broomstick Services
Ann Jungman

One day Joe, Lucy and Jackie find *three witches*
asleep in a shed. Aaargh!

The Marmalade Pony
Linda Newbery

Hannah has always longed for her very own pony.
But all she can do is pretend . . .

The Wishing Horse
Malcolm Yorke

Albert travels the land with a wise old man, and
together they grant *very* special wishes . . .

YOUNG HIPPO SPOOKY

Do you like to be spooked?
These Young Hippo Spooky stories
should do the trick!

The Screaming Demon Ghostie
Jean Chapman

Surely there can be *no such thing* as the Screaming
Demon Ghostie of the old forest track!

Smoke Cat
Linda Newbury

Every day, Simon sees something mysterious and
magical in next door's garden . . .

The Kings' Castle
Ann Ruffell

Claude haunts the Kings' castle. He lives behind a
wardrobe and likes to cause havoc!

Scarem's House
Malcolm Yorke

There's only one thing the O'Gool family can do
when their house is invaded by humans.
SCARE THEM OUT AGAIN!